The Feast in the Clouds

Patrick Okeke

AuthorHouse™
1663 Liberty Drive
Bloomington, IN 47403
www.authorhouse.com
Phone: 1 (800) 839-8640

Published by AuthorHouse 06/27/2019

ISBN: 978-1-7283-1717-5 (sc)
ISBN: 978-1-7283-1716-8 (e)

Library of Congress Control Number: 2019908712

Print information available on the last page.

This book is printed on acid-free paper.

authorHOUSE®

The story of the Turtle and how it got its broken
back as a consequence of cheating

Once upon a time Big Cats having lived in the clouds for 25 years decided to celebrate their Silver Jubilee with their friends by organizing a big feast in the clouds with their friends.

Invitations were sent out to all their friends

Hare, Fox, Birds, Turtles, other animal friends of theirs. Some of their friends cannot fly but they wanted them in there anyway.

Turtles received their invitation and were very excited about it. Hare, Fox and others were also excited about the invitation. All the animals invited have always enjoyed close friendship with the Bird community and were very excited to share this great invite with the Birds. When they called up the Birds they found out that the Bird community was also invited to the party.

Hare, Fox and Turtle community reached out to the Bird community indicating their interest to borrow some Feathers to enable them make the flight to the Feast in the Clouds. Fox and Hare request for some Feathers were rejected by the Birds because of years distrust between the Bird Community and the Fox and Hare community. However, the Turtle community had a better luck. Even though the Bird community had some reservation about the Turtles they were able to broker an agreement that the Birds will loan the Turtles their feathers and assist them in learning how to fly and in test flights to ensure that Turtles will be able to attend the party.

Turtles promised to build and equip Bird nests for the Birds in return for out fitting of the feathers and all the test flight training that the Birds will give them. Some of the Birds like the Parrots wanted this agreement in writing and finalized before their flight to this feast in ninety days. Their fear was based on the history of the crafty dealings of the Turtles.

To be fair the Turtles insisted that this agreement should be finalized after they get their feathers outfitted and a successful Test Flight. After the successful test flight the Turtles moved the goal post again.

They agreed that The Birds and Turtle Community agreement will be finalized as soon as they make their successful flight to the feast in the clouds.The Birds kept their part of the agreement they loaned and fitted the feathers on the Turtle and supervised a successful test flight in preparation for a successful flight to the clouds.

On the day of the party both parties successfully made it to the feast in the clouds. Everybody was excited to be there and were having a wonderful time.

As the party was winding down the Birds wanted The Turtles to finalize the terms of the agreement as agreed but the Turtles denied ever agreeing to the terms the Birds were claiming. They could not be persuaded by the Birds. When the Birds could not get anywhere with the Turtles they demanded and angrily took back the feathers they loaned to the Turtles and made their flight back to Earth leaving the Turtles behind.

Now the Turtles had a decision to make, now that the party is ended. Turtles sent word to there community on earth and shared their ordeal with their community on earth. After some strategy was discussed such as free falling to a particular space on their landing. A space that will soften the impact of their free fall from the clouds. Their community put out all kinds of shock absorbing apparatus.

Turtles landing was not as successful as they had expected. The Turtles Backs were Broken in Several pieces and had to be stitched back by some amateur hands. This is why all Turtles have a PATCHED back or what you can call a broken back. The Turtles learned many lessons and one of the lessons they learned is that Cheating does not pay.

CPSIA information can be obtained
at www.ICGtesting.com
Printed in the USA
BVHW020624050719
552676BV00019B/780/P

9 781728 317175